The Dragon Egg

Michelle Zimmerman

ISBN: 9781522091011

DEDICATION

To our twelve children and fourteen grandchildren, who provide an endless supply of story ideas...

When Ryan woke up one cold December morning, he noticed his window was covered with fluffy white stuff. Yawning, he got out of bed and looked outside. Snow! It looked like it had snowed ALL night! What a great way to start the winter school break!

"Tyler!" Ryan yelled. "It snowed! It snowed!" He went over to his younger brother's bed and pulled the blankets off. "Tyler, wake up!" Ryan said, loudly.

Tyler opened one eye, squinting, and then he opened the other.

"Ugh! What time is it?" Tyler asked.

"Time for you to get a watch! Now get up!" Ryan implored.

Tyler sat on the edge of his bed. “I’m up, I’m up,” he sighed. “Did you say something about snow?” He asked with his groggy morning voice.

Ryan ran to the window and pointed outside. “Look!” Ryan said, excitedly.
Tyler walked over to the window. “Holy Cow!” Tyler exclaimed. “Let’s go sledding!”

The two boys quickly got dressed and ran downstairs. They put on their coats, snow pants, and gloves, and pulled on their boots and headed outside.

Their home sat at the top of a hill. At the back of their house, the hill sloped downward 50 yards and ended at the woods. Their backyard was perfect for sledding!

Ryan and Tyler each grabbed the same sled from the garage. It was an orange plastic sled that was good for speed, so they decided to share.

The boys jumped on their sled, pushed off, and away they went! They raced down the hill, laughing all the way down. Tyler and Ryan both rolled off into the snow, but their sled kept going into the trees.

“Ryan, will you help me look for the sled?” Tyler asked.

“Sure!” Ryan said, helping him to his feet.

The boys wandered into the thick, snow covered woods, looking for the orange plastic sled.

A dozen yards into the woods, Ryan saw something orange up against a tree. “I think I found it!” Ryan yelled. Tyler followed Ryan further into the woods. As they approached the sled, Ryan saw something farther off in the distance, glinting like gold in the sunlight. He went deeper into the woods, mesmerized by the glittery sight.

“I got it!” Tyler yelled, shaking the snow off his sled.

“Tyler, come over here!” Ryan yelled, excitedly, walking toward the golden object. Tyler hurried over to his brother.

"Look at this!" Ryan said, pointing at the ground. There was a nest, made of branches! Hidden among the branches and snow, was a large golden egg!

"Whoa!" Tyler exclaimed. "What is THAT?" He wondered out loud.

"I don't know," Ryan said, "but it's amazing!"

“What kind of egg do you think that is?” Tyler asked.

“I have no idea,” Ryan said, bending down to get a better look. It was nearly as big as a football!

Ryan gently reached his hand out and lightly touched the egg. “It’s cold,” Ryan said.

Suddenly, the egg trembled. The boys jumped back. Then the egg was still again.

“Maybe the mother abandoned her nest. Or maybe something happened to her,” Tyler theorized.

“Maybe,” Ryan said. “I think we should take it home.”

“Me too,” agreed Tyler. “Let’s wrap it up in my coat to protect it until we get to the house.”

"Good idea," Ryan said.

Ryan carried the sled up the hill, while Tyler carefully carried the egg back to the house. By the time they reached the top of the hill, Tyler was tired. The egg must have weighed twenty pounds, but they didn't want to take a chance of it falling out of the sled.

When the boys reached home, they peeked in the window. Mom was in the kitchen, making breakfast. Both boys quietly opened the back door, and crept upstairs, as noiselessly as possible. Once they made it to their room, they laid the egg on Ryan's bed and closed the door behind them.

"Don't eggs need to be kept warm so they can hatch?" Tyler asked.

"Yeah, I think so," said Ryan. Suddenly, Ryan's eyes lit up. "Let's get mom's hair dryer and use it to warm up the egg!"

"Great idea!" Tyler said.

"Ryan! Tyler! Breakfast!" Their mother called upstairs.

"We'll warm up the egg after breakfast," Ryan told his brother.

The boys hurried downstairs. Their mother had made bacon and pancakes, and set juice on the table. Both boys wolfed down their pancakes in record time. They gulped down their orange juice, grabbed a few pieces of bacon and raced back upstairs.

Ryan pointed the blow dryer at the egg and began to heat it all over.

Thirty minutes later, the egg began to tremble again. Then it rolled to one side. The boys' eyes were wide with excitement. They put their ears close to the egg. They could hear a faint scratching sound. The egg rolled the other way. It began moving back and forth.

Without warning, a small piece of the egg flew off! Then another! The egg started cracking down one side, then along the top. A clear, gooey substance was dripping and oozing down one side of the egg.

Suddenly, a small creature popped its head out of the broken egg! It was green and scaly. It had sharp teeth, wings, and a tail!

Ryan and Tyler stared at the creature in astonishment. Their mouths had dropped open and their eyes were wide with amazement.

“Grabbukrek!” Shrieked the baby whatever it was.

“It looks weird,” Ryan said, “like... a dragon?”

“Yeah,” Tyler agreed. “Definitely a dragon.”

The little baby dragon took a step forward, and then fell. It shook itself off and stood up again on wobbly legs.

Ryan gently picked it up and said softly, "Hi, little guy."

"Groopkt," the dragon cooed back.

"Are you hungry?" Ryan asked. The little dragon took one look at Ryan's finger and bit it. HARD!

Ryan jerked back his finger. “Ouch! That hurt! We need to find you something else to eat besides ME!”

“What do you think it eats?” Tyler laughed at his brother. “Besides you?”

“I don’t know. Let’s see if he likes bacon,” Ryan suggested.

Tyler walked over to their dresser, where they had put their breakfast bacon, and broke a piece of it into bits. He put one bit down on the bed in front of the little dragon.

The dragon sniffed it and backed away, like he thought it was going to bite him. Then slowly, carefully, the dragon inched backed up to it. It lowered its head to it and sniffed again. The dragon opened his mouth and gobbled it up!

“Greebch!” The dragon screeched with enthusiasm.

"I don't know what he's saying. But I think he likes bacon." Tyler mused.

"I think you're right," Ryan said. The boys picked up all the pieces of bacon, and began giving them to the little dragon, one bit at a time.

"You need a name," Ryan said to their little friend. "How about..."

The dragon suddenly stopped and opened his eyes wide.

"What's the matter?" Tyler asked the little creature.

"Ah, Ah, CHOO!" The little dragon sneezed. Sparks of flame shot out of the dragon's nostrils. A few sparks even came out of his ears!

Ryan looked at his blanket, eyes wide in alarm. The dragon had burned a hole in his blanket!

“A fire-breathing dragon!” The boys exclaimed, simultaneously. “Wow!”

“Let’s name him Scorch!” Tyler said.

“That’s perfect!” Agreed Ryan.

Finding food for Scorch was easy. There were always plenty of scraps from the table, or things to warm up in the fridge. But the hardest part about having a dragon was keeping him QUIET!

Over the next several days, Ryan and Tyler took Scorch back to his nest, to try and find his mother. There were no tracks or any other signs around anywhere. She had simply disappeared.

During this time, Scorch grew quickly. It was amazing what the little dragon would eat! When the boys brought leftover food from the fridge, Scorch would blow some fire on it to warm it up, and then he would eat it. Scorch even ate Mom's leftover meat loaf, and no one ever eats that!

The winter break was going to end soon, and the boys had no idea what they were going to do with Scorch. They were afraid that if they told their parents, someone would come and take Scorch away. They thought about building him a shelter in the woods, but it was very cold. Scorch liked to snuggle up to them to keep warm, and the boys were afraid he would freeze in the woods, all by himself.

On the last day of winter break, Ryan and Tyler made one last trip to the forest with Scorch. They had to decide what to do with their little dragon.

"I think we should tell mom," Tyler suggested. "She'll know what to do."

"I just can't understand why a mother dragon would leave her little baby," Ryan sighed, as he played with Scorch. Their little dragon liked practicing his fire-breathing. The boys would toss a snowball into the air, and Scorch would try to melt it before it hit the ground.

Ryan had learned the hard way about making sure he was standing BEHIND Scorch before he tossed one into the air. Scorch burned the fringe off of Ryan's scarf one time, and nearly burned his hand on a different toss.

While the boys were deciding what to do, Scorch stopped shooting flames at their snowball tosses.

"What's the matter, boy?" Tyler asked.

Scorch was looking around him, like there was danger approaching.

The boys looked around, too, but they didn't see anything out of the ordinary.

"C'mon, Scorch," Ryan insisted. "Shoot the snowball!"

Ryan tossed one more into the air, and suddenly, it melted in a HUGE ball of flame! There was a loud crashing noise right above them, and a large shadow blocked out the sun. Ryan and Tyler both looked up and saw the largest, most fierce looking dragon ever! And it didn't look happy with them at all!

"RUN!" Ryan screamed, as he scrambled to his feet. "RUN!"

Both Ryan and Tyler ran for their lives through the forest. They went as fast as they could through the brush and the deep snow. Behind them, they could hear something very large and very fast crashing through the woods. The loud squawking and screaming was deafening! They could feel the tremendous heat, every time the beast shot fire at them.

“I think we found Scorch’s mom!” Ryan screamed, as he ran through the woods.

Tyler didn’t say anything. He was too busy running for his life!

The monster was catching up to them. The boys ran as far and as fast as anyone ever had, but they were just not fast enough to stay ahead of a very angry mother dragon. Finally, both boys fell, face down into the deep snow, exhausted and crying.

The large, angry dragon stood over them. She seemed in no big hurry to eat them, but she landed nearby and kept up the intense screaming. It was obvious that she was very mad at them for disturbing her nest.

As the monster approached, Ryan and Tyler rolled over to face the dragon. Just as she was about to shoot more fire, the boys were surprised by something else falling on them.

Little Scorch landed between the boys, with one of his little wings across each of them. Scorch faced his mother. He was shooting little fire balls and sparks at his own mom! Little Scorch was trying to protect them!

The angry mother dragon did not know what to do. She couldn't shoot fire at the boys, without hurting her own little dragon. Finally, she realized that Ryan and Tyler were his friends, and Scorch was not in danger.

Without another word, the mother dragon scooped up her little baby and flew away.

The boys, tired and sweating, sat up in the snow and looked at each other. Then they looked back at the sky, where the dragons had gone. Ryan started laughing. Tyler was laughing, too. Then they both stood up. They looked around, brushed off the snow, and headed for home.

Ryan and Tyler decided that no one would believe their story, so they never shared their secret.

Now you know the story about the golden dragon egg, and the real reason why Ryan’s blanket had a hole burned through the middle!

THE END

A personal note from the author-

If you enjoyed this book, please consider taking a few moments to leave a favorable review. Reviews help get the word out about this book, and are a great encouragement.
Thank you so much!

Other books by Kurt and Michelle Zimmerman can be found on Amazon.com

Printed in Great Britain
by Amazon